D1238679

Carmen

and
THE HOUSE THAT
Gaudí
Built

Written by
SUSAN HUGHES

Illustrated by
MARIANNE FERRER

OWLKIDS BOOKS

"Carmen Batlló,
our very important visitor
is here!" called Mercedes.
"Where are you hiding *this*
time? Come out!"

Dragon, Carmen's invisible salamander, didn't move.

Carmen didn't either.

Mama and Papa had bought a house on the fanciest street in Barcelona. And if the famous architect Señor Antoni Gaudí agreed to fix it up ...

"It will be the most *modern* house in Spain," bragged Carmen's sister.

"And we'll move to the city," her brother sang out.

No, no! thought Carmen.

But yes.

Mercedes paraded over to meet the architect. Juan raced full out. And now Papa, Mama, and Señor Gaudí were shaking hands.

Carmen stayed hidden.

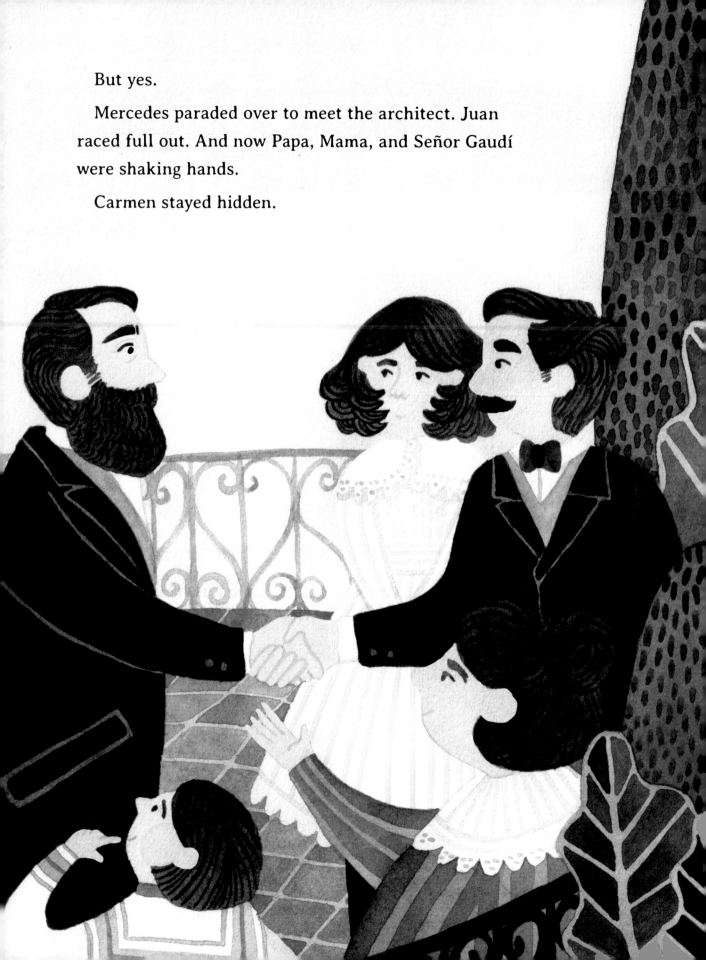

Yet somehow, Señor Gaudí
looked right at her.
And—was it possible?—
at Dragon too.

"I know you'll be fine here without me," Carmen told Dragon.
"The city is no place for salamanders."

But what would *she* do without her friend and the wild
beauty of the woods they roamed together every day?

In the woods, hollows cradled them close and hills tumbled them about.

Water sparkled and the light showed them colors everywhere.

Trees swayed, gently, fiercely.

Could Carmen ever feel at home in the gray, straight, stiff city? Impossible!

Months passed, and then Señor Gaudí visited again.

"This is our daughter Carmen—the one we can't keep inside," Papa said.

Señor Gaudí smiled. "I feel we've already met."

Carmen trailed behind as the adults walked.

"Sunshine is the best painter," marveled Señor Gaudí.

"We do not create," he said later. "We discover!"

The words swirled with possibilities. "But what," Carmen asked Dragon, "could this have to do with the new house?"

When Papa went to the city
to check on the renovation, he
invited Carmen to come along.

"Just to see," she told Dragon.

The two men inspected the
site. Carmen stood and stared.

Señor Gaudí invited Papa and Carmen on his daily walk.

And, oh! A park where this surprising man peered into burrows and examined spiderwebs. Picked up shells, pine cones, feathers. "There are no straight lines or sharp corners in nature," he murmured.

And Carmen understood. Señor Gaudí's words *did* have something to do with the new house!

After lunch, Papa looked over the architect's plans.

Carmen made drawings of her own.

"Ah, that's your friend," said Señor Gaudí.

Carmen blinked, then grinned. "Yes." In that remarkable way of his, Señor Gaudí saw so much. Even Dragon!

The next time Papa slipped away to Barcelona, Carmen asked if she could go too. And the next time and the next.

Carmen saw the house come alive.

Outside, mosaics sparkled. *Oh, like lilies floating on a rippling pond!*

Inside, Carmen ran her hands gently over the curving walls. She curled herself into their nooks.

"There are skulls and bones and yawns.
A mushroom fireplace. Swirls, whirls, and
sunbursts."

After every visit, Carmen's words painted
pictures of the house for Dragon.

"There are turtle shells. A well of light as
shimmery blue as under the sea."

Two years passed in this way, until ...

"Today we move to our new house in the city!" cried Juan.

"Carmen Batlló!" Mercedes called. "Where are you hiding *this* time?"

"I'll miss you,"
Carmen told Dragon gently.

Then, on the fanciest street in Barcelona, there it was. The most modern house ever—Casa Batlló. Finished now, inside and out.

The house was a wild beauty. And perched right up top, an amazing surprise.

Carmen smiled.
This house—this city—
could be a home for
her after all.

Author's Note

Antoni Gaudí, a well-known Spanish architect with a fabulously unique style, lived from 1852 to 1926. Seven of his works are UNESCO World Heritage sites, including the Basílica de la Sagrada Família, Park Güell—and Casa Batlló, the house in this story. In 1904, Josep and Amàlia Batlló, wealthy textile factory owners, gave Gaudí total creative freedom to redesign and renovate a house they had recently purchased in Barcelona. Sparkling, colorful, energetic Casa Batlló would become a masterpiece of architecture and design, and a home to the Batllós and their five children, including the youngest daughter, Carmen.

Although the interactions in the story between Gaudí and Carmen and her family are imaginary, the descriptions of the architect's ideas about design and beauty—although they seem fantastical—are based on facts.

Between 1904 and 1906, Gaudí redesigned the Batlló house with incredible care and attention to detail, bringing it to life with light and color, inside and out. He fashioned a house with few sharp corners or straight lines. He renovated the outside walls, making them wavy, and replaced all the inside walls, making them curved. He reshaped some exterior windows. And to fill rooms on every

floor with more light and air, he widened the inner courtyard to turn it into a light well, topped it with a skylight, and decorated the walls with about 15,000 tiles in five shades of blue. Gaudí even designed much of the furniture, including benches and chairs in natural shapes to fit against the curved walls.

When it came time to create the front mosaic, Gaudí stood outside the house and directed the placement of each colorful tile or glass fragment, one by one. Finally, he designed a spine-like ridge along a sinuous, scaly roof that looked remarkably like a dragon or a salamander! Why? Many believe he was recalling the legend of St. Jordi, who battled a dragon to save this region of Spain. But Gaudí himself never said. Which leaves plenty of room to imagine that he might have been influenced by young Carmen's longing for a home for herself and her imaginary salamander.

A statue of Antoni Gaudí sitting on a mosaic bench near Park Güell, in Barcelona. Behind him is a photo of his Basílica de la Sagrada Família. Begun in 1882, the remarkable building has been under construction for more than 135 years!

The spectacular Casa Batlló in Barcelona, designed by Antoni Gaudí, 1904–06.

SELECTED SOURCES

Bassegoda Nonell, Joan and Daniel Giralt-Miracle, Jaume Sanmartí Verdaguer. *Casa Batlló, Gaudí: Light & Colour.* Barcelona: Casa Batlló-Triangle Postals S.L., 2012.

Casa Batlló, Antoni Gaudí Modernist Museum in Barcelona, Spain. Online.

Grossman, Rachel. "Inside Casa Batlló." *Architecture Week: Design and Building in Depth.* Artifice, Inc. 13 Nov. 2002. Online.

Rodriguez, Rachel. *Building on Nature: The Life of Antoni Gaudí.* New York: Henry Holt and Company (BYR), 2009.

Text © 2021 Susan Hughes | Illustrations © 2021 Marianne Ferrer

All rights reserved. No part of this publication may be reproduced, stored in a retrieval system, or transmitted in any form or by any means, without the prior written permission of Owlkids Books Inc., or in the case of photocopying or other reprographic copying, a license from the Canadian Copyright Licensing Agency (Access Copyright). For an Access Copyright license, visit www.accesscopyright.ca or call toll-free to 1-800-893-5777.

Owlkids Books acknowledges the financial support of the Canada Council for the Arts, the Ontario Arts Council, the Government of Canada through the Canada Book Fund (CBF), and the Government of Ontario through the Ontario Creates Book Initiative for our publishing activities.

Published in Canada by Owlkids Books Inc.
1 Eglinton Avenue East, Toronto, ON, M4P 3A1

Published in the US by Owlkids Books Inc.
1700 Fourth Street, Berkeley, CA, 94710

Library of Congress Control Number: 2020939448

Library and Archives Canada Cataloguing in Publication

Title: Carmen and the house that Gaudí built / written by Susan Hughes ; illustrated by Marianne Ferrer.
Names: Hughes, Susan, 1960- author. | Ferrer, Marianne, 1990- illustrator.
Description: Includes bibliographical references.
Identifiers: Canadiana 20200259334 | ISBN 9781771473927 (hardcover)
Subjects: LCSH: Gaudí, Antoni, 1852-1926—Juvenile fiction.
Classification: LCC PS8565.U42 C37 2021 | DDC jC813/.54—dc23

Edited by Karen Li & Debbie Rogosin
Designed by Alisa Baldwin

Photo credits: page 30: © Sjankauskas/Dreamstime.com; 31: © Valery Egorov/iStock.com

Manufactured in Shenzhen, Guangdong, China, in September 2020, by WKT Co. Ltd.
Job #20CB0766

A   B   C   D   E   F

ONTARIO ARTS COUNCIL
CONSEIL DES ARTS DE L'ONTARIO
an Ontario government agency
un organisme du gouvernement de l'Ontario

Canada Council for the Arts   Conseil des Arts du Canada

Canada

Publisher of Chirp, Chickadee and OWL
www.owlkidsbooks.com

Owlkids Books is a division of bayard canada

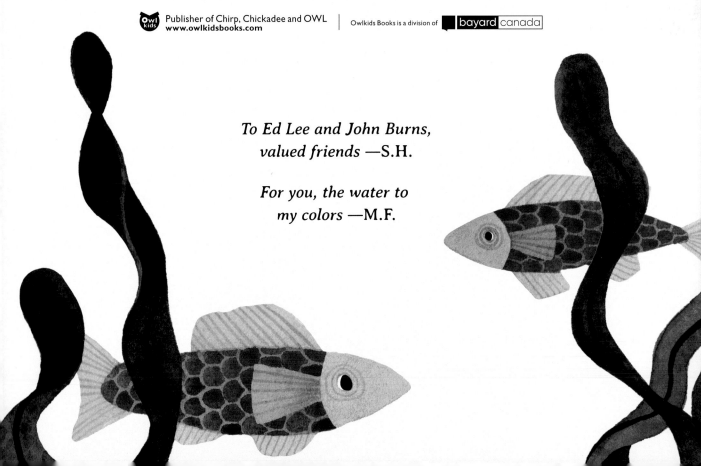

To Ed Lee and John Burns, valued friends —S.H.

For you, the water to my colors —M.F.